Dear faden

FOCUS ON THE FAMILY PRESENTS

THE IMAGINATION STATION®

D0959460

# Danger on a Silent Night

**BOOK 12**

**MARIANNE HERING • NANCY I. SANDERS**
**CREATIVE DIRECTION BY PAUL McCUSKER**
**ILLUSTRATED BY DAVID HOHN**

love
Uncle Rob
+
Aunt Deb

TYNDALE

**FOCUS ON THE FAMILY • ADVENTURES IN ODYSSEY**
**TYNDALE HOUSE PUBLISHERS, INC. • CAROL STREAM, ILLINOIS**

*Danger on a Silent Night*
© 2013 Focus on the Family

ISBN: 978-1-58997-739-6

A Focus on the Family book published by Tyndale House Publishers, Inc., Carol Stream, Illinois 60188.

Focus on the Family and Adventures in Odyssey, and the accompanying logos and designs, are federally registered trademarks, and The Imagination Station is a federally registered trademark of Focus on the Family, Colorado Springs, CO 80920.

TYNDALE and Tyndale's quill logo are registered trademarks of Tyndale House Publishers, Inc.

Cover design by Michael Heath | Magnus Creative

Cataloging-in-Publication Data for this book is available by contacting the Library of Congress at http://www.loc.gov/help/contact-general.html.

Printed in the United States of America
1 2 3 4 5 6 7 8 9 / 16 15 14 13

For manufacturing information regarding this product, please call 1-800-323-9400.

To Arman and Elham,

Just as the wise men did, you started your journey
in Persia. Then, oh glorious day! You found your Savior,
the King of the Jews. May God continue to bless
you with the joy of His presence as you share the
good news with others!

—NIS

# Contents

# Present Problems

Patrick's boots crunched in the snow on the sidewalk. He was on his way to Whit's End. His cousin Beth walked beside him.

Patrick's nose felt frozen. He clutched a small gift bag in his hand. It had a big red bow on it.

"I still think your decision is weird," Patrick said to Beth.

Beth shook her head. "Mr. Whittaker will understand."

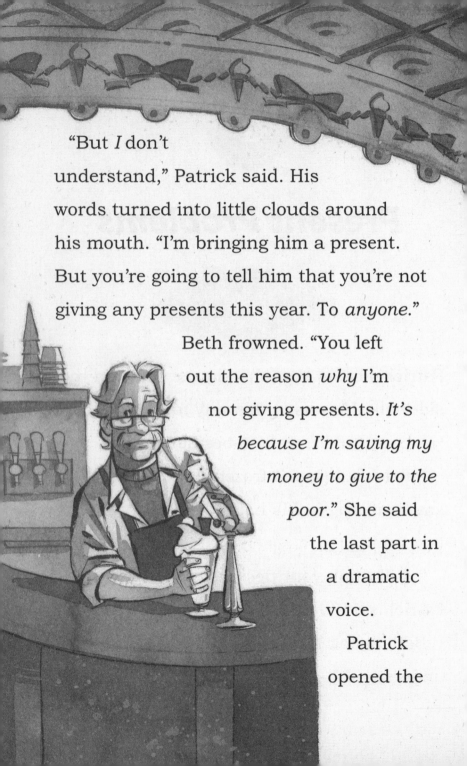

"But *I* don't understand," Patrick said. His words turned into little clouds around his mouth. "I'm bringing him a present. But you're going to tell him that you're not giving any presents this year. To *anyone*."

Beth frowned. "You left out the reason *why* I'm not giving presents. *It's because I'm saving my money to give to the poor*." She said the last part in a dramatic voice.

Patrick opened the

door to Whit's End. The bell on the door jingled as he stepped inside. Beth followed close behind.

Mr. Whittaker stood behind the counter. He was making a milk shake. He looked up and smiled. "Merry Christmas!" he said.

"Merry Christmas!" Patrick and Beth said together.

Patrick walked to the counter and held out the bag to Whit. "My mom baked these for you," he said.

Whit took the bag and looked inside. He closed his eyes and sniffed deeply. "I *love* gingerbread cookies. Thank you," he said.

"You're welcome," Patrick said. He glanced over at Beth.

Beth looked away.

"Do you mind if I share these?" Whit asked

Patrick. He put the gift on a shelf behind him. "If I eat them all myself, I'll gain weight. Then I might have to ask for a new belt for Christmas."

"Sure," Patrick said. "They're yours. You can do whatever you want with them."

The cousins took off their mittens and sat at the counter.

Whit busied himself with making mugs of hot chocolate. "Are both of you ready for Christmas?" he asked them.

"Almost," Patrick said.

"I am," Beth said.

Whit raised his eyebrows. "You've already done *all* your Christmas shopping?" he asked her.

Patrick looked at Beth to see how she would reply.

"I'm not shopping for Christmas this year," Beth said. "I'm not giving gifts."

"Oh?" Whit said.

Beth lifted her chin proudly. "I'm giving my money to needy families," she said.

Whit looked impressed. "Well, that's a sacrificial thing to do," he said.

"She didn't say she wouldn't *take* any gifts," Patrick said in a sharp tone. "She said she isn't *giving* any."

"I'm not asking for any gifts this year. I have told everyone not to give me gifts," Beth said. She frowned at Patrick. "I don't want any money spent on me. It should go to the poor instead."

Patrick looked at Whit. "Help me, Mr. Whittaker," he said. "What's it going to be like with no Christmas presents under the tree? It's crazy."

Whit rubbed his chin thoughtfully. "You don't always have to *buy* gifts," he said. Then he turned to Beth. "You could make something by hand—like decorate a picture frame or knit a scarf."

"I would still have to buy the supplies," Beth said.

Patrick put his face in his hands and groaned. "You can't have Christmas without presents. It's . . . it's . . . *tradition.*"

"It wasn't always tradition," Beth said. Then she looked doubtful and asked Whit, "Was it?"

Whit put some mugs of hot chocolate on a tray. "Let me deliver these drinks. Then I'll *show* you the answer," he said.

"Show us?" Patrick asked. Then he

realized what Whit was saying. "An Imagination Station adventure?"

Whit chuckled as he walked away with the tray.

Patrick looked at Beth. Beth seemed excited for a second. Then her expression changed to serious. "This won't change anything," she said firmly.

"Are you sure about that?" Patrick asked.

"You'll see," Beth said.

Whit led the cousins down a set of stairs to his basement workshop. They crossed the room to a large machine. It looked like the front of a helicopter. The Imagination Station! Patrick patted its side and felt the cool metal.

The Imagination Station was one of

Whit's inventions. It was kind of like a time machine. It let kids experience history for themselves.

Whit pushed a button, and the door slid open. The cousins climbed inside and sat in the seats.

Whit pushed several keys on the machine's control panel. The Imagination Station started to hum. Lights flashed on and off.

"I hope you enjoy yourselves," Whit said.

"What will this tell me about giving gifts?" Beth asked.

Whit smiled and waved. "Push the red button when you're ready," he said. The doors slid closed.

Patrick reached out and pushed the red button.

The Imagination Station started to shake. It seemed to move forward. Then it rumbled. Then it whirred.

Beth gasped.

Patrick felt the machine speed up. It zoomed along through a kind of tunnel. The tunnel seemed to get smaller and smaller.

Suddenly, everything went black.

# Magic!

Patrick felt a warm glow on his face. His nose wasn't cold anymore. He blinked at the sun. Then he looked around. He was sitting on a large rock. The ground was sandy at his feet.

The Imagination Station faded away.

*I forgot to ask Mr. Whittaker where we were going,* he thought.

Patrick wondered what kind of clothes he was wearing. He always found himself in different clothes in the Imagination Station. Maybe they'd give him a clue. He looked down. He was wearing thick robes with colorful embroidery. A heavy gold necklace hung around his neck.

He noticed a hat on his head. Patrick reached up and felt cloth. A wide strip of material was twisted like a cinnamon roll. *A turban*, he thought. He touched a large jewel attached to the front of it. It was about the size of a baseball.

He searched his pockets. Whit often gave him a small gift to use in each adventure. But his pockets were empty. *Did Mr. Whittaker forget to give me something?* he wondered.

He stood up and looked around. On Patrick's left was a large open field of sand. On his right stood a row of tall, thick bushes. A few were as tall as a man. Beth was nowhere to be seen.

Suddenly he heard voices coming from the other side of the bushes. They were *angry* voices.

*Uh-oh, I hope Beth isn't in trouble already,* he thought.

Patrick crept up to the bush. He spread apart some branches and peeked through the opening.

He saw two groups of men. They were standing on opposite sides of a hole in the ground. Square, flat stones lined the hole.

One group of men wore simple brown robes. A herd of twelve donkeys was gathered near them. Each donkey carried a large bundle on its back. The animals looked worn and tired. They only moved to twitch their ears.

The second group of men wore beautiful robes. Jewels decorated their clothes. The shiny gems looked like giant candy gumdrops without the sugar.

More than twenty camels stood around the men. Each camel was covered with a fancy blanket that looked like a carpet. Each blanket had dozens of long tassels. Patrick whistled to himself. These men had money. Lots of it.

The men in brown robes were different. He remembered drawings he'd seen of trading caravans in the Middle East. The men in brown robes looked like traders.

The shouting between the two groups grew louder.

One man in a brown robe stepped forward. His fists were clenched. Then a man from the other group came closer. He pointed to the hole.

Patrick guessed the hole in the ground was a well. The two groups seemed to be fighting over it. He scanned the crowds. He was hoping to spot Beth. But he saw only the men and their animals.

A man from the wealthy-looking group tossed his hands in the air. He looked disgusted. He shook his head and then turned and walked toward Patrick.

*Maybe he's seen Beth*, Patrick thought. He stepped out from behind the bush as the man approached.

The man looked surprised to see him there.

"Have you seen a girl with brown hair?" Patrick asked.

The man looked at Patrick with an odd expression. He shook his head. "A girl? No, of course I haven't," he said. "We travel only with men."

"What about them?" Patrick asked. He pointed to the other group of men.

"You'll have to ask them yourself," the man said.

Patrick looked at the arguing men. "What are they fighting about?" he asked.

"Our caravan has been traveling for days," the man said. "Our camels need water. But the traders say the well is theirs because they were here first. We said we'd be happy to take the water *after* them. But they insist we cannot have any water at all."

Just then, Patrick heard a man in a brown robe shout. That man shoved a man from the other group. The other man shoved back. A few other men began to throw punches. The argument was turning into a fight.

"Oh no," the wealthy man said to Patrick.

"What can we do?" Patrick asked.

Suddenly there was a loud *ka-pow!* and a bright flash of light. A thick cloud of white smoke exploded next to the bush.

Patrick jumped and stumbled away from the explosion. He bumped into the wealthy man. The man reached out to steady him.

Several donkeys reared back. The fighting stopped. Both groups of men turned to see what had happened.

Patrick saw a white cloud of smoke. As

the smoke thinned, a young man stepped forward. It seemed as if he had magically appeared. He wore a huge gold turban like a snail shell. His robes were made from shimmery fabric. He looked like a prince.

"Stop fighting, and share the water!" he called out. "There is enough for all!"

Then he raised an arm toward the sky and opened his hand. There was another *ka-pow!* and cloud of smoke. The young man vanished.

The men in brown robes were amazed. Some fell to their knees.

"Magic!" they cried with fear. "They have magic!"

# The Palace

Beth opened her eyes. She was now sitting on a low couch.

She stood up. She was wearing a long white dress. It felt like silk. She turned her head. Something else felt different about her. She put her hand on her head. Her hair was pulled back and fastened into a bun.

Beth quickly glanced around. She was in a large room made of stone and marble. A low table was against a wall. It reminded

Beth of a coffee table. Two chairs with
plump cushions were also against the wall.
Next to her was a tall golden screen with
tiny holes in it.

"Patrick?" Beth said.

"Who's there?" a voice called back. It was
a girl's voice.

Beth pressed her face against the screen.
She could see through the holes. A girl
stood on the other side. She looked older
than Beth.

"Come out where I can see you," the girl
said.

Beth stepped around the screen.

The older girl was wearing a long white
gown like Beth's. Her hair was pulled back
in a bun too. She held two long wooden
tubes that looked like flutes.

"You must be the new servant girl," the older girl said. "I'm Judith. What's your name?"

Beth smiled shyly and said, "My name is Beth."

"You're just in time, Beth," Judith said. She pointed at a small harp sitting on a table. "You may carry my lyre. I'm going to entertain the king."

Beth wasn't sure what to do. Where was Patrick?

"Hurry!" Judith said.

Beth picked up the lyre. It was heavier than it looked.

She followed Judith through a maze of dim hallways. The plaster walls were painted with pictures of grapevines. The marble pillars were draped with curtains.

Fancy clay lamps sat on ledges along the walls. The light glowed in the hallways.

Beth thought each hallway was more beautiful than the one before it.

The girls entered a large room. The walls were made of marble. Tall, majestic columns stood in rows. The floors were covered with brightly colored stones. They formed pretty pictures of winding vines.

Beth noticed a thin, old man at one end of the room. He wore a long white robe with wide purple trim. He sat on a large chair with a high back and white cushions. The throne was on a raised platform.

Several men were in the room. Some stood, lingering near the throne. Some rested on low couches. Most wore togas. Beth knew they were from ancient Rome.

*Am I in Rome?* Beth wondered.

Beth looked at the old man on the throne. He was talking to a man wearing a soldier's uniform. The soldier had a long, pointy nose. He reminded her of a rat.

"This way," Judith said. She led Beth around to one side of the throne.

Beth could hear the man's words as they came closer.

"It's the richest caravan I've ever seen, King Herod," the man said. "It came from the East. It's the talk of all Jerusalem."

King Herod's eyebrows shot up in alarm. His eyes darted wildly around the room. He placed his hand in front of his mouth. He leaned closer to the man and whispered something behind his hand.

"Rumors are that some in the caravan are

magicians," the rat-faced man said. "I was told they could turn ordinary rocks into gold!"

"What's going on?" Beth whispered to Judith.

"The king is holding counsel," Judith whispered back. Then she tipped her head toward the rat-faced man. "That man is Brutus. Stay away from him."

Brutus now noticed Beth and Judith. He stopped talking. His pointy nose twitched.

"Did Your Highness ask for music?" he asked. He glared at the girls.

"I did," the king replied. He waved to the girls.

Judith sat on the stairs near the throne. Beth sat behind her. Judith put the mouthpieces of both flutes in her mouth at once. She played a soft song on the wood instruments.

The king closed his eyes and listened. Brutus sneered and stepped away with a slight bow to the king.

The music sounded different from anything Beth had ever heard. It didn't follow rhythms or have a clear melody.

Beth looked around the room for Patrick. She didn't see him anywhere.

Soon Judith finished the song. Then she handed Beth her flutes.

Judith then took the lyre from Beth. She began to pluck at the strings. Beth wasn't sure she liked the music.

King Herod gestured to Brutus.

The man stepped forward.

"Enough," Brutus said to Judith. "The

king tires of music."

Judith stood and bowed. Beth imitated her. Then the girls turned and headed for the hallway.

"Wait!" a voice called out.

Both Beth and Judith turned. It was Brutus.

Brutus marched up to the girls. His helmet covered most of his face. But Beth could still see his eyes and nose.

He studied Beth. "Are you the new servant girl?" he asked. His nose looked even pointier up close.

Beth wasn't sure what to say. So she nodded.

"You were very watchful in the throne room," he said. "What were you looking for?"

"My cousin," she said.

"In the *throne* room?" he asked. "What cousin of a servant could be found in the throne room?"

Beth opened her mouth to speak.

But Brutus leaned toward her before she could say anything. "Where are you from?" he asked. "Are your parents Jews or Romans?"

Beth's heart pounded hard. She didn't know what to say.

"Sir, she was helping me," Judith said in a timid voice. "She was there only because I asked her to come."

"Is that so?" Brutus said. "What do you know about her? How can you be sure she wasn't hired to poison the king? Or slip a knife into his back!"

Beth gasped. "No!" she cried.

A bell rang from the throne room behind him.

Brutus frowned. "The king is calling me," he said. He pointed his finger at Beth and said, "I'm keeping an eye on you!" He turned on his heel and walked away.

Beth turned helplessly to Judith. "What am I supposed to do?" she asked.

Judith looked worried. "You'd better watch out."

# *Apellus*

Patrick watched the merchant traders stumble over themselves from fear. They dragged their animals away from the well.

"Take the water!" their leader said to the wealthy men. "Drink all you want!"

They hurried away from the water hole.

The rich men watched the merchants in the brown robes leave. Some of the wealthy men were smiling.

"That takes care of that," said the wealthy

man standing near Patrick. Then the man walked away.

The servants of the wealthy men walked to the hole. They were carrying strange-looking buckets. The buckets looked like they were made of animal skins. One at a time, the men lowered the buckets into the well.

Patrick wondered about the mysterious young man. He had suddenly appeared and then disappeared in puffs of smoke. But was it really magic?

The rich men didn't seem disturbed at all.

Then Patrick heard rustling from behind the bushes. He poked his head around the other side. He was surprised to see the young man standing there. He was brushing dirt and ashes off his fine robe.

The young man looked at Patrick and

smiled. "Did the men stop fighting?" he asked.

"Yes," Patrick replied. "Your trick scared them away."

"Good," the young man said. "It was selfish of them to refuse my people water."

Patrick looked around for evidence of the young man's trick. But he couldn't find any.

The young man gazed at Patrick. "Who are you?" the young man asked.

Patrick smiled and introduced himself. "My name is Patrick," he said.

The young man bowed. As he bowed, he touched his forehead and then his chest. "I am Apellus," he said. "I am the firstborn son of Datis, king of the wise ones."

Patrick bowed to the prince.

Apellus seemed to study Patrick. "You

dress like the people from my country," he said. "But you don't act like them. Are you from the East too?"

Patrick glanced down at his clothes. He said, "I'm not really sure which direction I'm from. I was with my cousin, and she got lost. Or *I* did. I'm not sure. I thought she might be by the well. But she could be anywhere."

"You're welcome to travel with us," Apellus said. "We are journeying to Jerusalem. Perhaps you'll find her there."

"Maybe you can make her appear with your magic," Patrick said.

Apellus smiled. "It's not really magic. Magic is dark and evil. My father would never allow it."

"Then how did you appear and disappear in the cloud of smoke?" Patrick asked.

"I'll tell you my secret if you travel with us," Apellus said.

"First I have to make sure my cousin isn't here," Patrick said.

"Then let's look together," Apellus said.

They moved out from behind the bushes and walked toward the well. The search for Beth didn't take long. There weren't very many places she could be. Patrick finally decided to travel with Apellus. There was nothing else he could do.

"Come with me. I'll find a camel for you to ride," Apellus said.

Patrick followed Apellus to a group of camels. Some were resting on the ground. Others were standing in a line. Still others were drinking water from a stone trough.

Patrick eyed the huge beasts. "I've never

ridden a camel before," he said.

Apellus looked at Patrick in surprise. "Do you travel by horse?"

"No. I usually ride my bike," Patrick said.

"I've never heard of that creature," Apellus said.

Patrick didn't bother to explain. "What about the camel?" he asked.

"It's not hard to ride,"

said Apellus. He guided Patrick over to one sitting on the ground. "This is Old Neb. Just climb on. He knows what to do."

Patrick frowned. The camel looked old and grumpy. "Will he let me?" Patrick asked.

Apellus chuckled. "Yes," he said. "I'll show you. Watch me." The young man climbed on a nearby camel.

Patrick swung his leg over Old Neb's back and onto the saddle. The camel groaned as he stood up. Patrick held on with both hands as the camel swayed back and forth. He was afraid he might fall off. It seemed like a long way down to the ground.

"Whoa, boy," Patrick said nervously.

Apellus laughed again. Then he reached under the camel's saddle blankets. He pulled out a long, thin branch. He flicked the branch on the camel's neck.

The prince's camel groaned and then stood up. Soon all the camels lifted themselves on spindly legs. Patrick wondered how the animals' knobby knees could support their giant hump.

The camels' loud noises also surprised Patrick. Their snorts, blats, and bellows sounded like out-of-tune tubas.

Apellus's camel moved forward, hump swaying. Old Neb snorted and then followed.

The prince's and Patrick's camels moved in line with the others. The caravan moved slowly out of the valley.

Patrick's camel climbed to the top of the hill. The camel groaned and complained all the way. Patrick looked across a field and saw a hillside covered with buildings. The city looked about a mile away.

"What is that city?" he called to Apellus.

"Jerusalem!" the young prince called back.

"What are we going to do there?" Patrick shouted.

"We're going to visit the royal palace!" Apellus said.

"What?" Patrick asked. "Why are we going there?"

Apellus called over his shoulder, "To find the newborn King of the Jews!"

# *Three Wise Men?*

"The newborn King of the Jews?" Patrick called. "Do you mean Jesus?"

"Jesus?" Apellus asked. He slowed his camel so Patrick could catch up.

"You know, Christ the Lord, the newborn King," Patrick said. "Like in the Christmas songs."

"I don't understand what you're saying," Apellus said. "But we know a new King has been born. My father tracked the star that marked His birth. That's why we've traveled here."

Patrick thought about this news for a while. Then he asked Apellus, "Are you carrying gold and myrrh with you?"

Apellus glanced at him. "We have gold and myrrh," he said. "And frankincense. They are gifts for the King."

Patrick rode on in silence. It was a lot to think about. He'd had many adventures in the Imagination Station. But he never expected to meet the baby Jesus. Or would he? He couldn't remember what happened to the wise men in the Bible.

The caravan passed through a grove of bushy olive trees. The air was dry and warm. The scent of olive oil made Patrick think of Italian food.

Finally, the caravan came to the gates of Jerusalem.

The city spread out over the hillsides. A gigantic stone wall surrounded it. Tall buildings towered above the wall. Their color and rectangular shape reminded Patrick of sand castles.

Old Neb stopped suddenly, and Patrick jerked forward. He grabbed the saddle with both hands. He felt himself slipping off. But he held on and soon settled himself again. He looked back at the long train of men and camels. He silently counted the number of men dressed in rich robes. *One, two . . . seven!* he thought. *It can't be!*

"Apellus! Who is your dad? And who are the men with him?" he asked.

Apellus answered, "They are the seven

wise ones from my country. Some would call them kings. My father is their leader."

"Not three?" Patrick asked. "There should be only three."

Apellus looked puzzled. He tapped his camel with the branch, and it stopped. Old Neb stopped too. The camels behind them came to a halt, too.

"What's this talk of *three* wise men?" Apellus asked Patrick as he climbed off his camel.

"I thought there were only three," Patrick said again. Old Neb let out a mighty groan. The old camel folded his legs and settled on the ground.

Patrick held on as his seat swung back and forth. He was glad to climb off. His back and legs felt stiff. "I guess the songs got it wrong," he said.

Apellus shook his head at Patrick. "Songs?"

"Never mind," Patrick said. "What are we doing now?"

"We're waiting for my father," Apellus said. "We shouldn't enter the city without a formal message to the king."

Patrick looked back at the caravan. *That could take a while*, he thought. "Will you tell me your secret while we wait?" he asked. "How did you do the trick at the water hole?"

The young man nodded. "I'll tell you," he said, "because now we're friends. But it wasn't a trick. It was *knowledge*."

"Knowledge?" Patrick asked.

"My father experiments with different salts, elements, and compounds," said Apellus. "He knows which ones to mix to create smoke. He knows which ones to mix to create light."

"Oh! You mean *science*?" Patrick asked.

At first Apellus looked confused. "Sigh-ants?" he asked. Then he smiled and said, "Oh, you mean *scientia*. That's Latin. Yes, that's exactly what I mean. Someday I hope to learn everything my father knows."

"How did you make the smoke?" Patrick asked.

Apellus held open his outer robe. Patrick saw many hidden pockets sewn inside.

"I simply mixed several salts and elements. I always carry pouches of them in my pockets," Apellus said.

Then he pulled a pouch out of a pocket. "I threw this mixture on the ground. When it made the cloud of smoke, I stepped into it. Nobody saw me until the cloud disappeared."

"Could you teach me some of your knowledge?" Patrick asked. "I'd love to show this to Beth."

"I'll teach you when we have time," Apellus said. "Right now my father is coming."

An older man walked toward them. He had a long white beard. He wore a green robe with white fur trim. A long green feather was on the top of his turban.

"My son," Datis said as he came close. He bowed slightly.

"Hello, Father," Apellus said. "This is Patrick. He's looking for his cousin. I invited him to travel with us."

Datis bowed to Patrick.

Patrick bowed too.

"Do you know where your cousin might be?" Datis asked.

"No," Patrick said.

Datis looked toward the palace. "Perhaps King Herod will know," he said.

"King *Herod*?" Patrick asked. Something about the name sounded familiar. He had a feeling it was something bad.

Datis said, "Herod has men watching his city. They report all news to him. He may have heard about your cousin."

Patrick gazed at the palace. He had a feeling that he would find Beth there.

"You may come with us to see King Herod," Datis said.

"Is that where we'll find the newborn

King?" Apellus asked.

Datis shook his head. "The star didn't place the Infant here. He was born in another town."

"Then why did you come here?" Patrick asked.

"To pay our respects to *this* king," Datis replied. "Come."

# *Only One King*

Patrick, Apellus, and the seven wise men walked through the city gate. Patrick saw Roman soldiers standing everywhere. Each wore silver armor and a silver helmet with a red crest. Many of them carried spears.

Patrick and the group from the East passed by more olive trees. They walked by a garden pond and through a courtyard. At the center of the pond was a bronze fountain. It spouted water in a high arc.

The wise men approached a tall stone tower. Its shape looked like a castle chess piece.

Two Roman soldiers opened a large door. A man in a plain white toga met them just outside the door.

"Welcome to King Herod's palace," the man said.

"We request an audience with the king," Datis said.

"I'll take you to him at once," the man said. "We've been expecting you."

They followed the servant through great passageways.

The halls were filled with wood furniture and large clay pots. The walls and doorways were covered with carved stone. Small tiles covered the floor. The footsteps of the wise men echoed with each step. The ceilings were high enough for a basketball game.

Then they entered a huge room with marble columns. A man sat on a throne in the middle of the room.

"Your Highness, your guests have arrived," the servant announced with a low bow. Then he turned to Patrick and the others. "I present King Herod!"

Datis and the other wise men knelt.

Apellus nudged Patrick. "Show some respect," the prince whispered.

Patrick flushed. Then he followed their example and knelt as well.

"We bring greetings, King Herod," Datis said.

A man appeared at Herod's side. The king whispered to him.

The man stepped forward. "I am Brutus, of the king's council. May we ask *who* brings greetings?" he said.

All the wise men stood. Apellus and Patrick stood too.

Datis said, "We come from the East, beyond the desert. We study the stars and seek wisdom from the God who created them."

Herod sat up in his throne.

"You are astronomers?" Brutus asked. "How interesting. Why do you honor our poor city with a visit?"

Datis said, "We have followed a star here. We believe this star announces the birth of a King. This King will be known as the King of the Jews. We have come to worship Him."

Patrick heard a sputtering noise and

looked toward the throne. Herod had stood.
His face was red with rage. He moved his
lips, but no sound came out. Then he sat
down and placed a hand over his mouth. He
leaned toward Brutus. Patrick could hear
Herod whispering.

"We have no knowledge of a King worthy to
be worshipped," Brutus said. "Herod is the
only king in this region we worship. He is
appointed by Caesar. *There is no other king.*"

There was an awkward silence. Datis
bowed low again. The green feather on his
turban touched the ground. "We are sorry to
have troubled you, great king," he said.

King Herod leaned forward and whispered
something to Brutus.

Brutus then said, "However, we would
like to hear more about this star and what it

means." He clapped his hands and shouted, "Drinks for our weary travelers!"

Servants suddenly entered from different doorways. They carried trays and pitchers. Some trays were filled with cheese and fruit. Other trays held goblets.

One girl came in carrying a large silver pitcher. It was Beth.

Patrick wanted to shout out her name. But he knew that would be dangerous.

Beth placed the pitcher on a table.

Patrick gave a little wave, but she didn't seem to notice him.

She turned and left the room.

"That's my cousin," Patrick whispered to Apellus.

Apellus didn't say anything, but he gave a slight nod.

Datis bowed to Brutus and the king. "Please forgive us for any disrespect on our part," he said. "We came merely as messengers. We have not bathed. Nor are we dressed in our finest clothes. We are not worthy to feast with you. Allow us to go and return in good time."

Datis signaled the others. Then he turned and walked away. Patrick, Apellus, and the other wise men followed.

*I'm not leaving this palace without Beth,* Patrick thought.

The group from the caravan came to a turn in the hall. And Patrick made his move. He ducked out of sight into a side passage. The others walked on without him.

Patrick waited until he was sure the hall was clear. Then he darted back toward the throne room.

A door slammed somewhere. Patrick looked around nervously. He quickly stepped into an alcove.

Footsteps came close and then faded away.

Patrick crept back into the hallway and hid behind a large stone pot. He had no idea where he was going. But he knew he had to find Beth. He decided to return to the throne room. Maybe Beth was cleaning up.

He carefully made his way to the large throne room door. It was closed shut. He leaned close to try to hear the king's voice.

Suddenly, rough hands reached around his face. They pressed hard against his mouth.

# *Simeon*

Judith and Beth waited in the servants' quarters. Beth sat on a low couch. She rubbed her face with her hands. *How long am I supposed to stay here?* she wondered.

Beth had been serving the king all day. She was either helping Judith with the lyre, or she was carrying in drinks for his guests. *Why has Mr. Whittaker sent me here?* she wondered. This palace didn't have anything to do with Christmas presents. Or with anything else she'd been talking about.

"You spoke of your cousin," Judith said.

"Patrick," Beth said.

"Did you see the boy who came with those men from the East?" Judith asked.

"No," Beth said. "What boy?"

"The others had dark skin," Judith said. "But a boy with pale skin was with them. He looked like you."

*That had to be Patrick*, Beth thought. She leaped to her feet. "I must find him!" she said.

"No!" Judith said sharply. "Brutus suspects you already. We can't let him find you walking around the palace alone. He might say you are a traitor and put you to death."

"Then what should I do?" Beth cried.

"Stay with me until everyone has gone to

bed," she said. "Then we'll find a way out of the palace. Maybe your cousin is still with the men from the East. If he is, we should find their caravan easily."

The evening passed slowly. Beth found it painfully boring. She plucked on the lyre while Judith practiced songs on her flute.

*Clang! Clang!*

"That's the king's bell," Judith said. "We must go back to the throne room." She grabbed her flutes and hurried down the hall. Beth followed behind her with the lyre.

This time King Herod was on his throne, and Brutus paced in front of him. But the throne room was filled with different men.

A group of men in plain robes stood in front of the throne. Most of them had dark hair and thick beards. One older man had a bushy beard. He was dressed in a light-brown robe. He held a large scroll in his arms. He looked nervous as he watched the king.

Judith suddenly stopped and gasped.

"What's wrong?" Beth whispered to her.

"That's Uncle Simeon!" Judith whispered back.

Simeon looked in their direction. He gave Judith a worried smile.

Brutus stepped between Judith and her uncle. "Yes," he said. "We've sent for your uncle."

"Why, sir?" Judith asked in a whisper.

"Because he is one of the best Jewish scholars in the city," Brutus said. "The king has need of his knowledge." Then he waved his hand past the other men. "The king has need of *all* his scribes and experts."

All of the men except Simeon bowed and
nodded. They muttered thanks for the honor
to be there.

"Then how may *I* serve you?" Judith asked.

Beth noticed that
Judith's eyes
remained
locked on
her uncle.

"Your
uncle is
fearful,"
Brutus said.
"The king believes
your music will
soothe him. It
will help him think

clearly while we discuss our business."

Judith looked at her flutes. She seemed unsure of what to do.

"Maybe if you play the lyre," Beth suggested. She handed the older girl the stringed instrument.

Judith's hands were shaking. "I'll try."

"Do better than try," Brutus said.

Judith sat on a large cushion near the throne. Beth sat at her feet. Judith began to play a gentle song on the lyre.

Music filled the room.

King Herod turned to Brutus. "Well?" asked the king. "Tell me about this infant King who dares to take my throne!"

Brutus's nose twitched. He turned to Simeon. "The Jews always have prophecies about everything. Surely there is one about a newborn King."

The dark-haired men gathered together and whispered among themselves.

Simeon raised his head. He said in a weak but clear voice, "The Roman emperor has appointed Herod king of the Jews."

Herod suddenly snorted. Beth thought it must be a laugh.

"He is avoiding my question," Herod said to Brutus. Then he shouted, "Tell me what you know, old man. Where will this so-called King be born?"

The room fell silent. Nobody spoke.

Brutus scowled and reached for his belt. He tossed a small bag on the floor.

*Clink!*

It sounded to Beth as if there were a lot of coins in the bag.

One of the scribes eyed the small treasure. He looked at the other scribes and then at the floor. He broke the silence by saying, "The prophet Micah has foretold the birth of a King. He wrote he would be born in Bethlehem of Judea."

The scribe went to Simeon. He took the scroll and unrolled it. The scribe searched through the scroll.

Then he began to read: "For this it is what the prophet has written:

'But you, Bethlehem, in the land of
    Judah,
are by no means least among the rulers
    of Judah;
for out of you will come a ruler
who will be the shepherd of my people
    Israel.' "

The scribe rolled up the scroll. He picked up the bag of coins from the floor. Beth watched him tuck it somewhere in his robes. Then he shoved the scroll back at Simeon.

King Herod rubbed his hands together. He whispered something to Brutus.

"Is that all?" Brutus asked the men.

They stood silent again.

Brutus clapped his hands. "Then go away!" he cried. "Leave at once!"

The scribes shuffled out like a row of penguins.

Brutus moved near the king. The two men talked to each other in low voices.

Judith and Beth stood and gathered the instruments.

"Follow me," Judith said. Beth obeyed.

Judith didn't go to their normal door.

Instead, she headed in the direction of her uncle. He was the last scribe to leave.

Simeon leaned close to Judith as they walked past him. "Meet me in the courtyard," he whispered.

Patrick struggled against whoever had grabbed him. Then a voice whispered in his ear, "Be still. It's me!"

The hands let go, and Patrick turned to face Apellus. "What are you doing here?" Patrick asked. He gasped, still frightened.

"I wasn't going to leave you alone," the young man said. "I intend to help you find your cousin."

"It's risky," Patrick said. "I hoped to sneak through the throne room somehow."

"We'll figure it out together," Apellus said.

"But what if we're caught?" asked Patrick.

"We're too clever for that," Apellus said with a smile.

Just then, the two turned around. For the second time, Patrick gasped.

Two Roman guards were pointing their spears at the boys' chests. "You're not as clever as you think," one of the guards said.

# The Lion of Judah

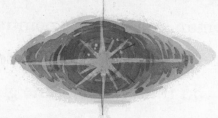

Judith led Beth back to her room. "There is a servants' passageway. It's on the other side of the throne room," she said. "We'll sneak you out that way."

Judith opened a small chest and began throwing clothes on the floor.

"What are you looking for?" Beth asked.

"A cloak for you to wear," she said. "You can't go outside dressed the way you are now." She held up a brown robe with a hood. She handed it to Beth.

Beth put it on. It was a little large, but a belt drew it close around her.

Judith looked her over. "Good," she said.

"Then where will I go?" Beth asked. She knew nothing about the palace or the city. And she wasn't sure she could find the baby Jesus.

"Follow the star," Judith said simply.

Beth was worried it wouldn't be that easy. How would she follow a star to the exact place?

"There's a hall that circles behind the throne room," Judith said. Then she stopped. "You're going to see the newborn King," she added.

Beth nodded.

"It is only right that you must take Him a

gift," Judith said.

Beth said, "I think I must have one . . ." She searched her pockets and clothes carefully. Certainly Mr. Whittaker had put something in her costume. He always did. But this time there was nothing. *I wonder if he forgot?* she thought.

Judith hurried to a small cupboard. The girl grabbed something and returned to Beth. "Give this to Him," she said. "It's a small toy lion I made for my nephew. I'll make him another one."

Beth took the toy. It was made out of rough fabric. She squeezed it. It felt as if it was stuffed with straw.

"A lion from Judith," Beth said. The phrase sounded familiar. Then she remembered and said, "The Lion of Judah."

Judith smiled. "Yes, the Lion of Judah is our promised King of Israel. He's been called 'the Lion of Judah' in our prophecies," she said.

Beth looked at the stuffed lion again. She felt a sense of wonder about all the prophecies. And she was there to watch them happen!

Judith handed Beth a leather pouch. "Put the lion in this," she said.

Beth slid the lion inside. Then she tucked the pouch in her belt.

"Now hurry!" Judith said. "I'll lead you out!"

# Herod's Lies

The two girls crept from Judith's room. They headed toward the throne room. They entered the servants' passageway. It was dark, and Beth had to feel her way along the wall.

They finally reached a door. "Is this it?" Beth asked.

"Not this one," Judith whispered. "That door leads to the throne room. Keep going."

But as they passed the door, Beth heard

voices. One of them was very familiar to her.

*Patrick!*

"I hear my cousin," she whispered to Judith.

"In the throne room?" Judith asked. She sounded worried. "But he left with the others."

"Something's wrong. He might be in trouble," Beth said. "Is there a way to sneak in to see?"

Judith groaned. "We could slip in through this door. Let's just hope no one sees us. The throne faces the other way. And there's a large statue we could hide behind."

"Let's try," Beth said.

They crept quietly into the room. Herod was on his throne talking to someone. Beth couldn't see who it was. The throne blocked her view.

"Why were you sneaking around the palace?" the king asked.

A voice Beth didn't recognize said, "My Lord King Herod, we were lost—"

"Don't lie to me," Herod said angrily. "You left with the other wise men *after* they refused my hospitality."

"We meant no disrespect," the voice said.

"I don't care what you meant. You came back," Herod said. "Why?"

"Honorable King—" the voice began again.

"Quiet!" Herod shouted. "I want to hear from the pale boy. He looks frightened enough to tell the truth. Speak!"

"I *will* tell you the truth," the boy said.

Beth gasped. It was Patrick's voice. How could she let him know she was there too?

"Then tell me the truth," Herod said.

"I'm not looking for a new King," Patrick said. "I'm looking for my cousin."

"Your cousin?" King Herod asked.

"Yes, sir," Patrick said. "I saw her earlier. She's a servant."

"Interesting," the king said. Then he was mysteriously silent.

Beth nudged Judith. "I have to be where I can see what's going on," she whispered.

"You'll be caught," Judith whispered back.

Beth pointed to another statue. "I can see from behind there," she said.

Beth pressed herself against the wall and edged toward the other statue. No one seemed to notice her.

She hid behind the statue and peeked out. She could see Patrick standing in front of the throne. Next to him was a young man dressed in colorful clothes.

"I'm a reasonable man," Herod suddenly said. "I might be able to help you find your cousin. I might also free you to follow that star. Isn't that what you both want?"

"Yes, sir," Patrick said.

"King Herod," the young man said.

Herod interrupted him. "You're a bold fellow to speak so freely to the king," he said. "What is your name?"

"Apellus, the son of Datis. My father is the leader of the wise men you spoke with," Apellus said.

Herod leaned forward. "Your father is the leader? Even better. Tell me, when did you first see the star?"

"My father discovered it nearly six months ago. He found it while he was studying the constellations," Apellus said. "It has taken us that long to travel here."

"And of course you came directly to me," Herod said. It didn't sound to Beth as if he believed it.

"It was only right to honor the king in Jerusalem," Apellus said. "This is the holy city of the Jews."

"You came to find the *next* King," Herod said. "But He isn't here. Our prophecies have declared that His birth will be in another place. Do you know where?"

Apellus frowned. "No. Our desire was to follow the star to wherever it led."

"The star will take you to the City of David," Herod said.

Suddenly Patrick said, "Bethlehem!"

"Yes," Herod said. "The scribes told me

that. You know our prophecies?"

Patrick shrugged and said, "A little."

Beth grew worried by this conversation. How much were they going to tell King Herod? If they said too much, he might find Jesus.

"Bethlehem?" Apellus asked. Then he turned to Patrick. "You know where the Child is?"

"Well, I don't have an exact address," Patrick said.

"This is what I'll do for you," Herod said. "I'll search for your cousin. I'll even allow you both to rejoin your caravan. But *only if* you report back to me. I must know where the Child can be found in Bethlehem."

Patrick and Apellus looked at each other. Beth could see from Patrick's expression that he didn't believe Herod.

Suddenly Herod added, "I want to worship Him too. Would you deny me that?"

Apellus bowed. "We'll most gladly obey you," he said.

"Then go to Bethlehem," the king said. "I'll find your cousin and send her to you. Does she have a name?"

"Beth," Patrick said.

Herod chuckled. "Like *Beth*lehem. How wonderful."

Patrick and Apellus bowed. Then they turned and walked to the waiting guards. Together they left.

Beth was about to sneak back to Judith when a door creaked. She froze where she stood. Brutus entered from a side door and approached the king.

"Well, Brutus?" the king asked.

"You handled that perfectly." Brutus said, sneering. "They'll lead us to the Child."

"What about the cousin? Have you found her?" the king asked.

"I sent guards to search the palace," Brutus said.

Beth was chilled to hear them talking about her.

"What should I do with her when we find her?" Brutus asked.

"Kill her," King Herod said.

"As you wish," Brutus said. He bowed and walked out.

The king stretched and then stepped down from the throne.

Beth could no longer see him. She pressed herself against the back of the statue.

Herod's footsteps paused.

*Is he looking at me?* Beth wondered. She didn't breathe.

Then the king grunted and shuffled out a side door.

Beth raced over to Judith. The poor girl looked ill. "Are you all right?" Beth asked.

"I've heard things I should not have heard," Judith said. Her eyes were wide, and her face was pale.

Beth put her hands on Judith's shoulders. She looked her friend squarely in the eyes. "I have to catch up with Patrick," she said firmly. "We have to get to Jesus before King Herod does."

Judith nodded. "This way," she said.

# The Secret Meeting

Judith led Beth to a stone bench in a far corner. The courtyard was like a small forest. There were lush potted plants, trees, and thick bushes everywhere. The bronze sculpture fountain in the courtyard bubbled with sparkling water. Beth couldn't believe people in Bible times made it work.

The girls sat down. A moment later, Simeon appeared. He had been hiding behind a large statue of a bird.

Judith leaped up and hugged her uncle. Then she introduced him to Beth.

Simeon seemed nervous as he looked around. "I'm sorry, but there is no time for long greetings," he said.

"What's wrong?" Judith asked.

"I have seen the Child they're looking for," Simeon said. "I even held Him in my arms."

Beth put a hand to her mouth.

"His name is Jesus," Simeon said. "He is the Messiah, the Savior of our people. He is our hope for salvation."

"You knew that from holding a baby?" Judith asked.

"I've waited my entire life to see Him," Simeon said. Then his brow creased with worry. "King Herod will kill the Child if he finds Him."

Beth reached out and gently laid her hand on Simeon's arm. "But Herod won't find Him. God will protect Jesus."

Simeon looked at her with surprise. "How can you know such a thing?" he asked.

"I know the story," Beth said. "Those wise men will follow the star. It will take them to the house of Joseph and Mary."

Simeon shook his head. "I don't know how you know the names of His parents," the old man said. "But if you're speaking the truth, you're in great danger. Herod would hurt you to find out what you know."

Beth put a hand to her mouth.

"Judith, you must get this girl away from the palace," Simeon said. "I'd take her with me, but that will attract the eyes of the guards. I came in alone."

"I'll find another way out," Judith said.

"I must go," Simeon said. He pulled Judith close for a hug.

"Good-bye, Uncle," she said.

"Good-bye," Simeon said. He let go of Judith and bowed to Beth. Then he slowly shuffled away.

"Now I'm even more afraid," Beth said.

"As long as Herod doesn't know—" Judith began to say.

Beth saw someone move in the shadows behind Judith. There was a rustling sound behind some potted trees. Judith turned to look. Whoever it was had gone.

"Brutus," Judith whispered.

"Did he hear us?" Beth asked in dismay.

"I don't know," Judith said. "But we must get you out of here."

"What about Patrick?" Beth asked.

"Do you want to risk the life of our Messiah to find your cousin?" Judith asked. She took Beth by the hand. "You must leave *now*. Go to the Child's house and warn them."

Beth didn't have time to protest. Judith pulled her across the courtyard.

# *Footsteps*

Beth followed Judith through the palace. They descended a steep flight of stairs. In a back room, a lonely door was tucked in a dark corner. Judith opened the door and then stopped to listen.

"What?" Beth asked.

"I thought I heard footsteps," Judith answered. "But they've stopped now."

Judith turned to face Beth. "This is as far as I dare go," Judith said. "Follow that alley.

It will lead you outside the palace grounds to the city. Make your way to the city gate. A large caravan from the East won't be hard to find. Ask anyone."

Beth hugged Judith. "Thank you for everything," she said.

"Don't forget to give the Baby my gift," Judith reminded her.

Beth touched the pouch on her belt. "I won't."

"God be with you," Judith said. Then she stepped back through the doorway. She pulled the door closed.

Beth looked up at the clear night sky. "God, please be with me," she said. Then she walked quickly up the alleyway.

Twice, Beth thought she heard footsteps as if someone were following her. But they seemed to stop every time she slowed.

She found a slave working in the olive grove. He told her exactly where the strange caravan was. She would find it just beyond the city gates.

Patrick waited outside a large tent. Apellus was inside the tent with his father. The prince was telling Datis everything that had happened with King Herod.

Patrick used the time to think. The story from the Bible came to his memory in pieces. He knew that Herod shouldn't be trusted. Herod was the kind of king who wouldn't give up his power easily. He would crush anyone who tried to take it.

A noise interrupted Patrick's thoughts. He turned toward the sound. A servant was pulling a girl by the arm. She was wearing a dark cloak. They were headed for Datis's tent.

"Stop it! Take your hands off me!" cried a voice. A *familiar* voice.

"Beth!" Patrick shouted. He saw that a servant was pulling her toward the tent.

"She was sneaking around," the servant said.

"I wasn't *sneaking*," Beth argued. "I was looking for Patrick and Apellus!"

"And here I am," Patrick said to the guard.

The guard let go of Beth's arm, bowed, and retreated.

Beth raced to Patrick and hugged him. Patrick kept the hug short, but he patted his cousin on the back.

"Are you all right?" asked Patrick. "I

didn't think Herod would let you go until we came back."

"He wasn't going to let me go. He was going to kill me," Beth said.

Patrick was shocked. "But he said—"

"Forget what he said. He lied to you and Apellus," she said. "I was hiding in the throne room when you met him. And I was there after you left. I heard his plans. We have to warn Mary and Joseph! Baby Jesus is in danger."

Patrick didn't know what to do about this terrible news. *Should I interrupt the meeting between Apellus and his father?* he wondered.

Just then, Apellus stepped out of the tent. He looked at Patrick. Then his gaze went to Beth. He bowed low and introduced himself to her.

Beth bowed too and gave her name. Then she quickly told Apellus what she'd said to Patrick. "Please," she said at the end, "we have to warn Mary and Joseph before it's too late! Herod's men will follow the star."

"Which star?" Apellus asked.

Patrick looked at him. "Which star?" he asked, confused. "The star you followed here."

"Look to the skies," Apellus said. "We haven't seen that star for a while. That's why we went to Jerusalem. We assumed it was guiding us there. Herod has told us otherwise. Now we'll have to search for the Child in Bethlehem."

"Really?" Beth asked. She was relieved. "There's no star for Brutus to follow? I thought the Bible said the wise men followed a star to Bethlehem."

Patrick looked up at the night sky. There were millions of stars shining. But they all looked the same to him. Patrick couldn't remember what the Bible said about the star. "So we don't have to worry about Herod and his men?"

"God is protecting Jesus," Beth said softly.

"We'd be fools to wait," Apellus said. "I have persuaded my father to take the caravan to Bethlehem. When we arrive, we'll see what we can find. You can ride with us."

"Ride?" Beth asked. She sounded worried.

Patrick grinned. "You get to ride Old Neb with me," he said.

"Who is Old Neb?" Beth asked.

"He's a camel," Patrick said. "His real name is Nebuchadnezzar, like in the Bible.

You'll like him."

"A camel?" Beth said. "You're not getting me on a camel."

"It's the only way to get there fast," Patrick said.

Apellus led them to the corral where the camels and horses were kept. Old Neb was resting on the ground. He let out a loud groan and puckered his lips.

Beth winced. "He looks like he's chewing on a sour lemon," she said.

"Watch out!" Patrick cried. He grabbed Beth's arm and pulled her away.

*Kersplat!* Old Neb shot a big glob of spit at them. It landed on the ground right where Beth had been standing.

"Ewww!" Beth cried.

Patrick and Apellus laughed.

"You want to watch out for camel spit!" Patrick said.

"It stinks too," Beth said, holding her nose.

"You'll get used to it," Patrick said. He climbed onto Old Neb's saddle.

Apellus helped Beth get on behind Patrick. Old Neb groaned, snorted, and bellowed.

"Hold on!" Patrick shouted. He and Beth swayed back and forth as the old camel stood up.

The rest of the caravan was ready. Patrick was amazed how such a large band of men could pack up so fast.

Apellus mounted his camel, too. "It's about an hour's ride," he said.

Within minutes, the caravan was headed down the road. They were on their way to Bethlehem.

By camel, an hour would seem like three hours. And it was late.

Old Neb soon fell to the end of the caravan. The beast's slow rocking motion made Patrick sleepy. Once or twice Patrick felt Beth's head bump his back. He wondered if she'd dozed off.

Patrick pulled a small pouch out of Neb's saddlebags. It held figs and cashews Apellus had given him. He shared them with Beth.

Old Neb followed the caravan down the dusty road. It was cold. Patrick stretched. His neck was a little stiff. He turned it to the left and right to loosen it up.

A moment later he thought he heard something behind him. He turned in the saddle to look. Beth jolted upright.

"What's wrong?" Beth asked. "Are we there?"

"I think someone is following us," he said, peering back into the darkness.

Beth spun to look. "I don't see anything."

Apellus brought his camel to a slow walk to allow them to catch up. "Do you see?" he asked.

"What?" Patrick he asked.

Apellus pointed to the sky.

Patrick and Beth looked. There, shining brighter than all the other stars, was *the* star.

"It's leading us to Bethlehem," said Beth

with awe.

Patrick felt a
flash of hope. But it
quickly faded. "If we
can see it, then Herod's
people can see it too."

"But we have an advantage,"
Apellus said. "We're ahead of
them."

Patrick looked back. "We're not as far ahead as you may think," he said.

Apellus followed his gaze. "Is someone there?"

Beth groaned. "Brutus could have followed me from the palace. I led him to you. And now we're leading him to Jesus."

Patrick peered into the darkness behind them again. "What are we going to do?" he asked.

Beth suddenly brightened. "I have an idea!"

# The Baby Jesus

"This way to the newborn King!" Beth shouted. Patrick and Apellus had agreed to her plan to break away from the caravan.

Apellus was on his camel up ahead. Patrick and Beth urged Old Neb to a gallop.

"Hurry!" Apellus called back over his shoulder.

Beth tried hard not to look behind them. They would lead Brutus on a wild-goose chase. They'd head toward the star and then away from Jesus.

"I hope this works," Patrick said.

"We only need to stall for time," Beth said. "The caravan has to get there first. Then Brutus won't dare to hurt baby Jesus."

Beth's heart beat like a wild drum. The three raced through the darkness. Soon the shadows of a village appeared in the moonlight. They were near Bethlehem.

Apellus and Patrick urged their camels on. Beth hoped that Brutus was following them. They raced down one street. They raced down another street. Beth looked back but couldn't see anyone.

"Is he following?" Patrick asked.

Beth was afraid they'd made a mistake. "I don't think so," she said.

Then suddenly, a rider on a horse

rounded a hut. Beth caught a glimpse of a soldier's helmet in the moonlight.

"Yes!" she said. "He's coming!"

Then Beth realized he was gaining on them fast. The caravan of men wasn't there to protect them now. Brutus certainly wouldn't be afraid of two kids and a teen.

"He's catching up!" Beth said loud enough for Apellus to hear.

Apellus slowed his camel. "Get in front of me," he cried out.

Patrick pushed Old Neb forward.

Apellus trailed along behind them. Beth saw him reach into a bag. He pulled his hand out and threw something over his shoulder.

*Ka-pow!* A thick cloud of white smoke suddenly appeared. Flashes of light filled the street behind them.

"That will slow him down!" cried Apellus. He pushed his camel faster and retook the lead. He turned his camel down a different street. Old Neb galloped after him.

They raced down more streets. They darted around corners. Finally the two camels came to a stop.

Apellus held open his outer robe. He reached into its pockets and pulled out two small leather pouches. He handed them to Patrick. "If these powders are mixed together, they explode," he said.

"Be careful. They're dangerous."

"I'll be careful," Patrick said. He tucked the

pouches in his belt.

Beth was still worried. "How do we find Jesus?" she asked. "We're as lost as Brutus."

Apellus looked at the bright star in the night sky. He seemed to be thinking hard. "This way," he said.

They followed Apellus down several narrow streets. Dark houses stood on either side. A man appeared in a doorway. He gave the travelers a curious look.

They turned the corner and came to an open field. A house stood in the middle of it. Lamplights flickered. Then Beth noticed that a caravan of camels surrounded the house.

"My father is here," Apellus said. They nudged their camels on. They arrived just as men with torches were dismounting their beasts. Beth saw a tall feather on one of the men's turbans.

"Father!" Apellus said.

Apellus's camel and Old Neb knelt for their riders to get off.

The men gathered at the doorway. Datis came over to Apellus.

"How did you get here so fast?" Apellus asked. "We sprinted ahead of the caravan. We should have been way ahead of you."

Datis smiled. "Once the star appeared in the sky," he said, "I knew exactly where it would lead us." He put his hand on Apellus's shoulder and said warmly, "You never studied properly."

"It's a good thing this time," Apellus said. "One of Herod's men was following us. We think we've lost him."

"I hope so," Apellus's father said.

Apellus quickly introduced his father to Beth. Datis bowed. Beth curtsied.

Just then, a servant approached. He handed Datis a small brown dish. A flame burned inside it.

Datis and the other wise men went to the door. Each of them carried a small box. The boxes were gold and covered with jewels.

Apellus stood next to his father. Datis signaled to a man nearby. The man handed Apellus a chest made of gold.

Beth and Patrick joined the wise men.

Beth gasped with excitement. "Is this it? Are we going to see the baby Jesus?"

Patrick put a hand on her arm and shook his head.

"What's wrong?" Beth whispered.

"They all have gifts, and we don't," Patrick

whispered back.

"I have a gift," Beth said. She reached into her belt and brought out a pouch. She pulled the stuffed toy lion out of the pouch. "Judith gave it to me."

Patrick smiled. "It's better than nothing," he said.

Beth looked at the gift and suddenly felt unhappy. "It doesn't seem like much," she said.

"Does it matter?" Patrick asked. Then he teased Beth and said, "Or would you rather sell this gift? You could give the money to the poor."

Beth scowled at him.

A man holding a lamp

appeared in the doorway. He looked as if he'd just woken up. He stared at the crowd with a puzzled look on his face. "I'm Joseph," he said. "What do you want?"

Datis stepped forward. "We have come from afar to honor the infant King."

Joseph stood silently for a moment. He glanced around at the group that had gathered. Then he nodded as if he understood. "Come in," Joseph said and stepped aside.

The wise men filed through the door. Beth and Patrick followed behind Apellus.

Beth was caught in the wonder of the moment. But she hadn't forgotten the warning she had to give Joseph.

The house was a little room with one small window. The window was nothing more than a hole in the wall with bars across it. The walls looked as if they were made of mud. Bundles of clothes, straw, jars, and bowls lay on the floor. Beth was surprised there wasn't any furniture.

She looked through a rear doorway. A donkey was standing in a stall. It munched on a bale of hay.

Joseph set his lamp on a ledge carved into the wall.

Beth saw a woman on the other side of the room. She knew it was Mary. Mary was sitting on a mat. She held a baby in her arms.

Mary smiled at the visitors. She put her finger to her lips. "Shhh," she whispered, "He's sleeping."

The wise men and Apellus knelt and began to whisper in a different language.

Beth realized they were worshipping the Child.

Patrick knelt. Beth took off her cloak and laid it on the floor. Then she knelt next to Patrick.

"I don't know what to say," Patrick whispered.

Beth nodded. It was one thing to worship God at church. It was another thing to kneel before Jesus and worship Him.

Datis stood and said, "Now we present these gifts to honor the newborn King."

The group of wise men set their boxes on the dirt floor.

"Thank you," Joseph said. His eyes were filled with tears.

Beth stepped forward. "Patrick and I brought a gift for Jesus too," she said,

stammering. "He's my cousin. Patrick, I mean. And Judith made the gift. She's Simeon's niece."

The Baby suddenly stirred, wiggling. Mary laughed softly. She looked up at Beth. "Would you like to hold Him?" she asked.

"May I?" Beth asked. She handed the toy lion to Patrick. Then she sat on a basket.

Mary picked up Jesus and put Him in Beth's arms.

Beth realized Jesus wasn't a newborn. She guessed that He was a few months old. His face was the most beautiful she'd ever seen.

Then He scrunched up His tiny face. *Waa-aaa!* Jesus cried. His face turned bright red.

"What do I do?" Beth asked in a panic.

Patrick knelt down. "Look here, Jesus," he said. "We brought You a toy." Patrick held the stuffed lion out to Him.

Baby Jesus stopped crying. He reached out His little hand and grabbed the lion. He waved the lion in the air. Then He smiled and gurgled.

Everyone laughed.

Beth couldn't believe she was holding Jesus in her arms. She felt like laughing and crying at the same time. She leaned over and kissed His soft cheek. The Baby gave a toothless grin.

Beth sighed with joy. Then she handed Jesus back to Mary.

She turned to Patrick with a smile as she stood up. The window was beyond Patrick's shoulder. To her horror, she saw a face looking in at them.

It was Brutus!

# Trapped!

Patrick was watching Mary and the Baby. Beth tugged at his sleeve. She looked upset. "What?" Patrick whispered to her.

"Brutus was at the window," she whispered back.

Patrick looked, but no one was there. "Let's make sure," Patrick said. He walked through the men to get through the door. Beth followed.

Brutus rounded the corner on foot as they

stepped outside.

"There!" Beth said.

Brutus saw the cousins, spun on his heel and ran.

Without thinking, Patrick said, "After him! We can't let him get back to Herod!"

Patrick and Beth raced after Brutus.

Brutus dodged down a narrow street. The cousins followed. Brutus pushed over large empty water pots to slow them down. Patrick and Beth had to dodge the broken fragments.

Brutus turned onto another street. Patrick and Beth raced after him.

They found themselves in an alley. A high wall was in front of them. It was a dead end. Where was Brutus?

Patrick noticed barrels and baskets in

the alley. He thought about stacking them. Then he and Beth could climb over the wall. He picked up an empty barrel.

Just then, Brutus leaped out of a doorway behind Patrick and Beth.

Patrick hadn't thought about what to do if they caught up to Brutus. He hadn't made a plan. Now they were trapped!

Brutus held a dagger in his hand. His mouth was drawn into a sneer. His pointy nose crinkled upward.

Patrick tipped the barrel and rolled it toward Brutus. But Brutus easily stepped out of the way.

Patrick moved to protect Beth.

Brutus stepped closer. "Your King can't save you," he said. "There is only one king in Israel. And he wants to be rid of you."

Just then Patrick remembered the pouches. He whispered to Beth, "Close your eyes." He grabbed a pouch from his belt and slammed it on the ground. It spilled open. Then he threw the second pouch.

*Ka-pow!* A thick cloud of white smoke shot up from the ground. Flashes of light exploded in front of Brutus.

The Roman stumbled back against a wall. He dropped his dagger. "Ahhh!" he cried out. He pressed his hands to his eyes.

Patrick grabbed Beth's arm. He pulled her through the smoke.

Strong hands clawed at the cousins. "I hear you!" Brutus snarled.

"Let me go!" Patrick shouted. He tried to pull away. But the grip on his arm was too tight.

"If I find that dagger . . ." Brutus said.

"There! That's where the light came from!" Apellus's voice shouted from the end of the alley. Several servants were with him.

Brutus let go of Patrick and rubbed at his eyes. "You dare not touch me," Brutus said.

Apellus snorted. "Bind him!" he said to the servants. They obeyed. Soon Brutus was sitting on the ground tied up with ropes.

"What will you do with him?" Beth asked.

"Let me go!" Brutus shouted. "The king—"

One of the servants wrapped a scarf around his mouth and cut off his words.

Apellus looked around. "Put him in that basket," he commanded the servants. "That will keep him out of trouble until my father comes. He'll decide what to do with him."

# The Vision

The night sky faded to dawn. The little town of Bethlehem began to wake up. Donkeys pulled carts along the streets, and camels carried bundles of goods.

Beth nudged Patrick, who was sitting in front of her on Old Neb.

"Look," she said. "The caravan is leaving."

The wise men and their servants were on camels. They slowly walked away from Joseph and Mary's house.

Apellus shouted for them to hurry up. Soon Old Neb was trotting alongside Datis's camel. The leader of the wise men sat tall on his camel. The feather in his turban swayed in the breeze.

"What's happening, Father?" Apellus asked. "Where are we going?"

Datis looked serious. "We're going home," he said. "We did what we came to do."

"What about King Herod?" Apellus asked. "He's expecting you to return to Jerusalem."

Datis shook his head. "Last night I had a vision," he said. "God warned me not to return to Herod. The king is evil and wants to kill the Child. He will do everything in his power to stop the rival King."

"He'll send his soldiers after us," Apellus said.

"We'll divide the caravan and travel by different roads," Datis said.

"What about *him*?" Apellus asked his father. He gestured to a cart with a large basket on the back.

"Is that the one you chased?" Datis asked.

Apellus nodded.

"We'll take him part of the way with us," Datis said. "Then we'll let him go at a safe distance from Jerusalem. By the time he returns to his king, it won't matter."

"What about Mary and Joseph?" Beth asked. "I still need to warn them."

"They are in the hands of their God," Datis said.

Patrick turned to Beth and said, "I think we should go back to make sure they're safe."

Beth nodded.

Apellus looked to his father. "May I join them?"

His father glanced at him. "If you must," he said. "But hurry to catch up. You don't know the route we'll travel. I don't want you to get lost."

Patrick and Beth said their farewells to Datis. Then, with Apellus, they made their way back to Joseph and Mary's house.

The boys tended to the camels after they arrived at the house.

Beth knocked on the door. No one answered. She walked to the side and looked in the window. The house was empty.

"They're gone," she said to Patrick and Apellus.

She looked toward the town. People were

going about their business. But there was no sign of a man, a woman, and a small child.

"I hope they go to a safe place," Apellus said. "Far away from Herod."

"Is Egypt far enough?" Patrick asked.

Apellus gazed at him. "Why do you think they'll go to Egypt?" he asked.

Patrick shrugged without answering.

"Your gifts will pay their way," Beth said.

Apellus thought about it for a moment. Then he nodded. "So they will," he said.

Just then, Beth heard a familiar hum. Patrick and Beth looked around to see where it was coming from.

"Is something wrong?" Apellus asked. He watched them closely.

"It's our way home," Beth said carefully.

Then she realized the sound was coming from *inside* the house. Suddenly the door to the house opened on its own.

"There," Patrick said.

"We have to leave you now," Beth said to Apellus.

Apellus looked puzzled. "If you must," he said and bowed low. "May your journey be safe," he said.

"Yours too," Patrick said. "And may you become the wisest wise man ever."

Apellus smiled.

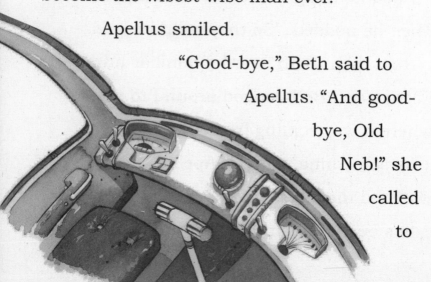

"Good-bye," Beth said to Apellus. "And good-bye, Old Neb!" she called to the camel.

The old camel grumbled. He puckered his lips.

Beth giggled.

Apellus didn't move. He watched the cousins walk into the house. "Wouldn't the *road* be faster?" he called after them.

Beth and Patrick smiled and waved without answering. They shut the house door.

The Imagination Station was inside. The cousins took their seats. Patrick pushed the red button.

The doors slid closed and everything started going black. As the blackness grew, Beth saw the door to the house open. Apellus poked his head inside and peeked at them.

# The Workshop

The doors of the Imagination Station slid open. Beth and Patrick saw Whit standing by his workbench. He was waiting for them.

The cousins got out of the machine. They were in their normal clothes again.

"So how did you like going back to see part of the first Christmas story?" Whit asked.

"Seeing Jesus as a baby was amazing," Patrick said.

"I got to hold Him!" Beth said.

"Did anything surprise you about those Christmas events?" Whit asked.

Patrick thought about Apellus and his father. "I was surprised about how many wise men there were. Who were they?" Patrick asked.

"The Bible doesn't say much about them," Whit said. "Some experts think they were descendants of Daniel."

"Daniel? You mean the guy from the Old Testament? The one who was thrown into the lion's den?" Beth asked.

"That's right," Whit said. "Daniel had been captured by King Nebuchadnezzar long ago. Daniel was taken to live in Persia. He became the leader of all the magicians and wise men there."

"Was Daniel a magician?" Patrick asked.

Whit shook his head. "No," he said. "Daniel knew better than to mess around with magic. The law of Moses forbade it. And Daniel was a faithful man. He trusted in God to give him all he needed."

Patrick nodded. "That sounds like something Apellus said. Though I don't think Apellus believed in God like we do," he said.

"We don't know for certain," Whit said. "But Christians traveled to that part of the world soon after Jesus rose from the dead. They preached the good news to the people there. And many became followers."

"I want to think that Apellus did," Beth said.

"And what did you learn about giving presents at Christmas?" Whit asked them.

"I felt bad that I didn't have a gift for the baby Jesus," Patrick said. "I mean, besides the little stuffed lion. But that wasn't really mine to give. It means more when I work to buy the gift. Or when I make it myself."

Whit nodded. "That's interesting. What about you, Beth?"

She paused for a moment and then said, "I felt the same way. Judith's gift was nice, but it didn't come from *me*."

"So do you think people should give presents at Christmas?" Whit asked her.

"I don't know," she said. "The wise men gave Jesus gifts. But the first Christmas wasn't really about presents."

"What was it about?" Whit asked.

"First, it was about Jesus," Beth said. "We spent a lot of time and energy looking for Him. The presents came second, as a way to honor Him."

"It sounds like you got things in the right order," Whit said.

Patrick thought for a moment. "Did the idea of giving gifts start with the wise men?"

"Some historians think so," Whit said. "Gift giving isn't about spending. It's about showing love and honor, just like Beth said.

Whoever we give to, we should give from the heart. We shouldn't give just because it's expected of us. Or because we expect to receive something in return."

"So it can work the other way around," Beth said.

"What do you mean?" Whit asaked.

"We show needy families love and honor by helping them," Beth said. "And because we do that, they might see Jesus."

Whit raised his eyebrows. "That's a good thought," he said.

"Wait a minute," Patrick said. "Is that the answer from our adventure? I'm confused."

Whit chuckled. "The apostle Paul said we should do everything to give God glory. Even eating and drinking. We can help the poor *and* give gifts to our loved ones. We don't have to choose between the two."

"I should think about giving more to help the needy," Patrick said.

"I want to show my family that I love them," Beth said. "So a few gifts wouldn't be wrong."

Whit smiled at them. "So you got your answer after all," he said. "Now let's go upstairs to the Whit's End Christmas tree. I forgot something in that last adventure, didn't I? I think there are a couple of gifts with your names on them . . . "

# Questions About the Wise Men

**Q: Were the wise men Christians?**

A: The Bible calls them, "Magi from the east," (Matthew 2:1). They had good astronomy skills and were willing to worship the Jewish God. They recognized the Spirit of God in a vision. The Bible doesn't say if they ever became followers of Jesus.

**Q: Didn't the wise men (not Apellus) meet with Herod a second time?**

A: Apellus is a make-believe character. To make the story more interesting for those who know it, we replaced the wise men's second meeting with Herod with a visit from Patrick and Apellus. See Matthew 2:1–12 for the whole story.

For more info on the wise men and Jesus' birth, visit *TheImaginationStation.com*.

# Secret Word Puzzle

Answer the questions, and fill in the clues. If you need help, look for hints on the pages listed.

**1** Scribe who believed Jesus was the Messiah: ___ ___ [ ] ___ ___ ___

(page 83)

**2** The country Daniel was taken to live in:

___ ___ ___ ___ ___ [ ]  (page 129)

**3** This guided the wise men to baby Jesus:

___ [ ] ___ ___  (page 52)

**4** The direction the wise men came from:

___ ___ ___ [ ]  (page 58, 88)

**5** One of the gifts the wise men gave:

___ ___ ___ ___ [ ]  (page 41)

**6** This king was angry about Jesus:

____ ☐ ____ ____ ____ (pages 52, 83)

**7** Jesus was the newborn King of this group of people:

____ ____ ☐ ____ (page 52)

Write the letters from the boxes, in order, in the boxes below. The answer is the secret word. It's also the name of the book of the Bible where you can read about the wise men.

| 1 | 2 | 3 | 4 | 5 | 6 | 7 |
|---|---|---|---|---|---|---|
| ☐ | ☐ | ☐ | ☐ | ☐ | ☐ | ☐ |

**Go to TheImaginationStation.com**
*Find the cover of this book. Click on "Secret Word." Type in the correct answer, and you'll receive a prize.*

**AUTHOR MARIANNE HERING** is the former editor of *Focus on the Family Clubhouse®* magazine. She has written more than a dozen children's books. She likes to read out loud in bed to her fluffy gray-and-white cat, Koshka.

**ILLUSTRATOR DAVID HOHN** draws and paints books, posters, and projects of all kinds. He works from his studio in Portland, Oregon.

**AUTHOR NANCY I. SANDERS** is the bestselling and award-winning children's author of more than eighty books. She and her husband, Jeff, rode a camel at the zoo. Find out more about the her at *nancyisanders.com*.